This one's
for Harry
P. H.

For P & P
Love D

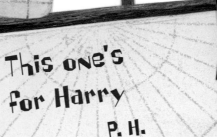

The Night Pirates

By PETER HARRIS

Illustrated by

DEBORAH ALLWRIGHT

SCHOLASTIC PRESS / NEW YORK

Down
down
down

the dark dark

street they came.

Quiet as mice,

stealthy as shadows.

Up up up

the dark dark house
they climbed.

Stealthy as shadows,

quiet as mice.

Only the moon
was watching
when they arrived.

Only the moon
was watching
when they left.

Only the moon . . .

. . . and one little boy.

Tom was a nice little boy.
Tom was a brave little boy.
Tom was a little boy about to have an adventure.

Who were these shadows
as quiet as mice
stealing away with
the front of Tom's house?

Maybe monsters
or trolls?

Maybe ogres
or gremlins?

Maybe
bandits
or pirates?

PIRATES???

PIRATES!

Rough, tough little girl pirates.
With their own pirate ship.

A ship set for sailing.
A ship off on adventures.
A ship stealing the front
of Tom's house
for disguise!

But what about Tom?
Could he join the crew?

"Please let me aboard!
Can I come, too?"

And did the girl captain say,
"Certainly not!
You're only a boy!"

Oh no, not at all!
Instead she roared,

"WELCOME ABOARD!"

Then up went the sails
and up went the flag.

Then off sailed the rough,
tough little girl pirates.

The little girl pirates
and their shipmate, Tom.

But where were they going?

To an island.

Where Captain Patch
and his rough, tough
grown-up pirates
were snoozing around their
full treasure chest.

Then Captain Patch saw something.

Something very strange.

Something very strange indeed.

What could he see?

A house,

sailing toward them,

coming closer.

"I've seen a house!" Captain Patch declared.
"We've all seen houses," said the pirates. "Who cares?"

"Don't just lie there. **Do something!**" Captain Patch roared.
But the pirates went back to sleep and just snored,
while the house sailed nearer and nearer until . . .

. . . out leapt
the girl
pirates!

Out leapt Tom!
And out leapt
a fearsome roar!

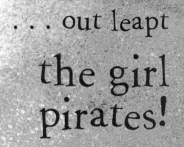

The pirates gaped.

The pirates goggled.

Then the pirates all ran away!

So Tom a[nd]
the girl pirat[es]
sailed off wi[th]
the treasu[re]
while the roug[h]
tough grown-[up]
pirates h[ung]
in the tre[es.]

Captain Patch stamped his feet
and shouted his worst pirate curse,

"If you don't give me
back my treasure,
I'll tell my MOMMY!"

But off they sailed,
all the way home.

Down
down down
down
the dark dark
street they came.

Quiet as mice,
stealthy as shadows.

Up up up

the dark dark house
they climbed.

Stealthy as shadows,
quiet as mice.

Only the moon
was watching
when they arrived.

Only the moon
was watching
when they left.

Only the moon
and one little boy.

Tom was a brave little boy.

Tom was a sleepy little boy.

Tom was a boy who had had an adventure.

And no one would ever find out . . .

. . . would they?

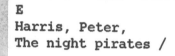